To Chad

ATHENEUM BOOKS FOR YOUNG READERS
An imprint of Simon & Schuster Children's Publishing Division
1230 Avenue of the Americas, New York, New York 10020
Copyright © 2019 by Brian Pinkney
ATHENEUM BOOKS FOR YOUNG READERS is a registered trademark of Simon & Schuster, Inc.
Atheneum logo is a trademark of Simon & Schuster, Inc.
For information about special discounts for bulk purchases, please contact Simon & Schuster Special Sales at 1-866-506-1949 or
business@simonandschuster.com.
The Simon & Schuster Speakers Bureau can bring authors to your live event. For more information or to book an event, contact the
Simon & Schuster Speakers Bureau at 1-866-248-3049 or visit our website at www.simonspeakers.com.
Book design by Ann Bobco
The text for this book was set in Kidprint.
The illustrations for this book were rendered in acrylic and India ink on Canson paper.
Manufactured in China
0419 SCP
First Edition
2 4 6 8 10 9 7 5 3 1
Library of Congress Cataloging-in-Publication Data
Names: Pinkney, J. Brian, author, illustrator.
Title: Puppy truck / Brian Pinkney.
Description: First edition. | New York : Atheneum Books for Young Readers, [2019] | Summary: Carter gets a truck instead of
a much wanted puppy, but he soon discovers his new toy is just as fun and rascally as a pet.
Identifiers: LCCN 2018020562 (print) | LCCN 2018028156 (eBook) | ISBN 9781534426887 (eBook) | ISBN 9781534426870 (hardcover)
Subjects: | CYAC: Trucks—Fiction. | Pets—Fiction.
Classification: LCC PZ7.P63347 (eBook) | LCC PZ7.P63347 Pu 2019 (print) | DDC [E]—dc23
LC record available at https://lccn.loc.gov/2018020562

puppy
truck

BRIAN PINKNEY

atheneum

ATHENEUM BOOKS FOR YOUNG READERS

New York   London   Toronto   Sydney   New Delhi

Carter wanted a puppy.

He got a truck.

So he pet it and
put a leash around it.

Vroom beep bark!

He led the truck to the park.

Vroom beep **bark!**

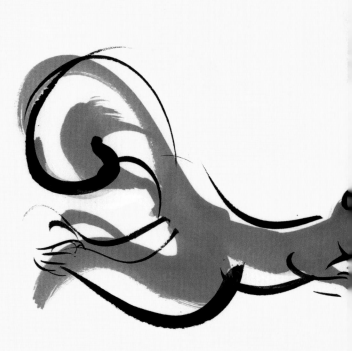

Vroom
beep
bark!

Mmm, my **Puppy Truck!**

Vroom beep bark!

So Puppy Truck led the way . . .

VROOM

They were so dirty,
they went home and had a wash.

splish
splash

They were so hungry,
they ate some nuts and bolts.

Chomp
chomp
Chomp munch

They were so tired,
they parked for the night.

Vroom beep zzzzz
Vroom beep zzzzz

The next day . . . .

Vroom beep bark . . .